My Brother's Famous Bottom

This is my mum.

This is my dad.

And this is my brother, Cheese. He's the one with the famous bottom.

Why is it famous? Well, it all started when . . .

Jeremy Strong once worked in a bakery, putting the jam into three thousand doughnuts every night. Now he puts the jam in stories instead, which he finds much more exciting. At the age of three, he fell out of a first-floor bedroom window and landed on his head. His mother says that this damaged him for the rest of his life and refuses to take any responsibility. He loves writing stories because he says it is 'the only time you alone have complete control and can make anything happen'. His ambition is to make you laugh (or at least snuffle). Jeremy Strong lives next to a volcano in Somerset. He has two cats and a flying cow.

www.jeremystrong.co.uk

Books by Jeremy Strong

MY DAD'S GOT AN ALLIGATOR!
MY GRANNY'S GREAT ESCAPE
MY MUM'S GOING TO EXPLODE!
THERE'S A PHARAOH IN OUR BATH!
LET'S DO THE PHARAOH!
THE HUNDRED-MILE-AN-HOUR DOG
RETURN OF THE HUNDRED-MILE-AN-HOUR DOG
THERE'S A VIKING IN MY BED
DINOSAUR POX

Jeremy Strong

My Brother's Famous Bottom

Illustrated by Rowan Clifford

PUFFIN BOOKS

To Susan, with love and thanks for all our time together

PUFFIN BOOKS

Published by the Penguin Group
Penguin Books Ltd, 80 Strand, London WC2R 0RL, England
Penguin Group (USA) Inc., 375 Hudson Street, New York, New York 10014, USA
Penguin Group (Canada), 90 Eglinton Avenue East, Suite 700, Toronto, Ontario, Canada M4P 2Y3
(a division of Pearson Penguin Canada Inc.)
Penguin Ireland, 25 St Stephen's Green, Dublin 2, Ireland (a division of Penguin Books Ltd)
Penguin Group (Australia), 250 Camberwell Road, Camberwell, Victoria 3124, Australia
(a division of Pearson Australia Group Pty Ltd)
Penguin Books India Pvt Ltd, 11 Community Centre, Panchsheel Park, New Delhi – 110 017, India
Penguin Group (NZ), cnr Airborne and Rosedale Roads, Albany, Auckland 1310, New Zealand
(a division of Pearson New Zealand Ltd)
Penguin Books (South Africa) (Pty) Ltd, 24 Sturdee Avenue, Rosebank, Johannesburg 2196, South Africa

Penguin Books Ltd, Registered Offices: 80 Strand, London WC2R 0RL, England

www.penguin.com

First published 2006
2

Text copyright © Jeremy Strong, 2006
Illustrations copyright © Rowan Clifford, 2006
All rights reserved

The moral right of the author and illustrator has been asserted

Set in Baskerville MT
Typeset by Palimpsest Book Production Limited, Polmont, Stirlingshire
Made and printed in England by Clays Ltd, St Ives plc

Except in the United States of America, this book is sold subject to the condition
that it shall not, by way of trade or otherwise, be lent, re-sold, hired out, or otherwise
circulated without the publisher's prior consent in any form of binding or cover other than
that in which it is published and without a similar condition including this condition
being imposed on the subsequent purchaser

British Library Cataloguing in Publication Data
A CIP catalogue record for this book is available from the British Library

978–0–141–31978–0
0–141–31978–X

Contents

Contents

1 The Big Plan

My dad's got a Big Plan. He told us all about it
at a special family meeting. All of us were there
– Mum, Dad, Granny and her husband,
Lancelot, me and the twins, even though they're
only one and a bit.

Dad banged a big spoon on the table to get
our attention and made
his announcement.

'We need a Big Plan,'
he told us.

'A big flan, dear?' said Granny. She's a
bit deaf and gets the wrong idea sometimes.
'What kind of flan? Strawberry? I like
strawberry flan. As long as it's not gooseberry,
or Marmite.' Granny pulled a face. 'Marmite
flan is horrible.'

I stared at Granny. What was she going on about?

'It's nothing to do with flans,' shouted Dad. 'I said we need a Big Plan.'

'Oh,' smiled Granny. 'I thought a big flan seemed silly, but then so many of your ideas are silly, aren't they, Ron?'

'You're so kind, Mother dear,' Dad said icily.

Mum sighed. Dad frowned and pulled at his beard. 'We have money problems. And the money problem is – we don't have any. We've nothing in the bank. In fact we have less than nothing in the bank.'

'Dad, how can you have less than nothing?' I asked.

'It's called an overdraft, Nicholas,' Lancelot explained. 'It means your mum and dad owe the bank money.'

'Exactly,' grunted Dad. 'It's because Cheese and Tomato cost so much.'

Mum glared at
Dad. 'How many
times do I have to
remind you that the
twins are called
James and
Rebecca, not
Cheese and
Tomato?'

Granny shook
her head. 'I don't
know what the
fuss is about. After all, they were born in the
back of a pizza delivery van. You should see the
faces my friends pull when I tell them my two

newest
grandchildren
are called
Cheese and
Tomato.'

'I don't want your friends pulling faces,' snapped Mum. 'Grannies are supposed to say things like "cootchy cootchy coo" to babies, not "ooh, cheese and tomato, my favourite, yummy yum"!'

'Whatever they're called, they cost too much,' grumbled Dad. 'They eat too much. They need too many clothes and they get through far too many nappies. They are costing us a fortune.'

'They can't go round without clothes or nappies, Ron,' Mum pointed out.

'I know that. I'm simply saying that we need to do something.'

'So, have you got an idea for a Big Plan?' asked Mum.

Dad smiled triumphantly. 'I have. In fact I have thought of several ways we can either make money, or save money.' No wonder Mum looked worried. Dad's plans for anything usually lead to trouble.

'OK,' he announced. 'Here is my first idea for making money: we sell the twins.'

'You can't sell Cheese and To– I mean, James and Rebecca!' protested Mum.

'It's only a suggestion,' said Dad hastily. 'Don't get your knickers in a twist. I can see you don't like that plan and I'm not very fond of it either, so here is my second idea: we sell Nicholas.'

'Dad!' I yelled.

'You don't like that either? OK, quieten down. You'll love this next one, I promise. Idea number three: we sell Granny.'

'Oh for heaven's sake, Ron, will you stop trying to sell off the entire family and come up with some halfway decent suggestion? And you can stop looking at me like that. I am not up for sale.'

Dad glanced round the table. He flashed his eyebrows up and down.

'Do stop grinning like that,' said Granny. 'You look like a cannibal wondering how tasty we might be to eat.'

'What an excellent idea,' said Dad. 'That would save us buying food for ages. We could eat each other. Who shall we start with?'

'YOU!' everyone shouted in chorus.

'Aagh!' Dad gave a startled jump back. 'All right, I get the message. Quieten down and listen because I do actually have a Big Plan. We're going to start a farm.'

YOU!!!

2 What Do Cows Lay?

My dad's always thinking up fantastic ideas and I thought this was one of his best. The others didn't seem nearly as excited as I was though. They just stared at him in stunned silence.

'Phew! You'll need more than a bit of dosh to start a farm,' Lancelot pointed out.

'And I don't want to move house,' said Mum. 'I like this house.'

'Me too,' I murmured. Under the table I crossed my fingers. I didn't want to move.

'No, no,' protested Dad. 'We're staying here. This place will be the farm.'

'That's the most stupid idea you've ever come up with,' declared Mum.

'We could have a mini farm,' Dad pressed on, 'with just a few animals, and we could grow our own vegetables.'

'That's what we did in the war,' said Granny. 'We had such fun. I was only a little girl, of course, but we had vegetables and chickens and rabbits.'

'That's it,' nodded Dad. 'We are going to grow as much of our own food as possible. In fact I shall grow some chickens too.'

Mum rolled her eyes. 'You can't grow chickens.'

'Yes, you can,' said Dad. 'You plant eggs and they grow into chickens, and you have to pick

them before their legs get too long and they run away.'

See? I said Dad has fantastic ideas. He's great! 'Anyhow,' Dad went on, 'the chickens will lay lots of eggs. And we could have a cow. What do cows lay, Brenda?'

'Cowpats,' said Mum, 'and you're talking nonsense. The garden is too small for a cow.'

'How about a goat then? We could get a small goat and every morning you could go out and shake it and get butter from it and cheese and milk and cream.'

'You have some very strange ideas about farming,' said Mum. 'Come to think of it, you have some very strange ideas about everything.'

'All part of my charm,' smiled Dad.

'I know how to milk a cow,' announced Lancelot.

Granny patted his arm. 'Lancelot is very clever with his hands,' she said.

'We're not having a cow,' repeated Mum.

Lancelot nodded. 'I know. But it works on goats too. I could teach Nicholas how to milk the goat.'

'Urgh! I don't want to milk goats.'

'Lancelot and I could take the milk to our house and make it into yoghurt and cheese,' suggested Granny.

'You should have some sheep,' said Lancelot. 'You could knit things then.'

'I think chickens and a goat will be quite
enough to start with,' Mum murmured.

'Are we really going to get chickens and
goats and everything?' I asked, getting quite
excited.

'Oh yes,' said Dad. 'And a rhinoceros.'

Mum sighed. 'Just ignore him, Nicholas.'

'Yes, ignore me, Nicholas,' said Dad. 'Go and
dig the vegetable patch instead.'

Did I say my dad's great? I've changed

my mind. Sometimes he can be very *un*great.

'And before you do any digging you can change the babies' nappies,' smiled Mum.

'Thank you,' I scowled. 'I'm just your slave really, aren't I?'

'Yes,' they answered.

I turned round to find the twins and of course they'd vanished, hadn't they? They're always disappearing. I think they do it deliberately. I tracked Cheese down eventually in Mum and Dad's bed. He was pulling Dad's pyjama trousers over his head, saying, 'Big dark! Nighty nighty!'

And what about Tomato? She was sitting in Mum and Dad's wardrobe, on the second shelf. *The second shelf!* How on earth did she get up there? She was pulling out Mum's T-shirts and throwing them all over the floor. So not only did I end up changing their nappies, I had to tidy the bedroom too and put everything back. Like I said, I'm just a slave really.

Anyhow, I'm really excited about the farm. It's going to be brilliant!

3 Twins in a Spin

I can milk a goat! I can! It's totally squirty!
Lancelot taught me. I didn't want to at first. It
felt so kind of icky and I got goosebumps just
thinking about it. Then I watched Lancelot do
it and it looked quite easy, and I thought if
Lancelot can do it then I can too. I mean, he's
sixty-six and he used to be a Hell's Angel and
he still has a ponytail and a leather jacket with
fringes and studs *and* he's got a monster
motorbike.

I sat down on a chair and Lancelot showed
me how to hold the goat's teat and squeeze the
milk out and I squeezed – and it worked! Wow!
I almost fell off my chair. I've got quite used to
it now and I think Rubbish likes it when I milk
her because she's always pleased to see me. We

call her Rubbish because she'll eat anything. She ate my shoelaces this morning.

When the bucket is full Granny and Lancelot take it to their house and put it in a big plastic tub. They're making it into yoghurt.

And you should see our garden too. Dad's planted

vegetable seedlings all over the place – potatoes, tomatoes, beans, spinach, lettuce, marrows – all sorts. And we've got ten chickens and a cockerel, not to mention Rubbish and a tortoise.

'Why do we have a tortoise?' I asked Dad.

'Couldn't get a rhinoceros,' said Dad. 'And he's our Chief Security Officer. He'll make sure the chickens stay in at night and he'll scare away any foxes. His name is Schumacher.'

Anyhow, we've had big excitement today, what with the twins vanishing (again), and our next-door neighbour, Mr Tugg. (More of the Terrible Tugg later.)

So, first of all Cheese and Tomato disappeared. We couldn't find them anywhere. Mum was going bananas. 'Why didn't you keep an eye on them, Ron?'

'I was trying to stop the goat eating the washing.'

'Why didn't you keep an eye on them, Nicholas?'

'I was upstairs on the computer. Besides, I'm not their bodyguard.'

Then Dad made a big mistake. He asked Mum why *she* hadn't noticed the twins disappearing.

'Maybe it was because your lovely new cockerel came into the house and tried to roost halfway up the chimney,' she said. 'And after that your lovely cockerel tumbled back down the chimney, bringing half a ton of soot with him, and flew about the room merrily throwing it into

every possible

corner. And

after *that* I spent the

next hour cleaning up – all because

of your stupid, brain-dead cockerel!

You go and check the coal shed.

Nicholas, you search upstairs.'

We raced round for a bit, calling out and
bumping into each other, but we couldn't find
them anywhere.

'We'll have to call the police,' said Mum at
last, ashen-faced.

'Not again,' muttered Dad. 'We only rang
them last week about the twins vanishing.
They'll start thinking we're useless parents.'

Mum fixed Dad with a steely glare. 'Some of
us here *are* useless parents,' she said. Ouch!

'What about asking Granny and Lancelot if
they've seen them?' I suggested.

'Don't be silly, Nick. I know they can toddle quickly, but they don't even know the way to Granny's house.'

'Maybe they've learnt to map read,' Dad muttered, and I hid a smile.

At that moment there was a loud roar from outside, and a screech of tyres on the gravel. Talk of the devil! It was Granny and Lancelot, out on their monster bike. They had the sidecar with them – and strapped in were Cheese and Tomato, wearing mini crash hats and sunglasses!

'My babies!' cried Mum, scooping them into her arms.

'Wheeeee,' laughed Tomato.

'Wee wee!' echoed Cheese, and he did. Mum hastily put him down.

'Took them for a spin,' said Lancelot, with a big, crinkly grin. 'They gurgled all the way – loved it. I reckon they're going to be biker babes.'

'They are *not* going to be biker babes,' declared Mum.

'Oh, they'd look lovely in leather jackets and shades,' said Lancelot. 'Go on! They could have tattoos and everything.'

Mum gave a horrified shriek. 'Tattoos! Don't you even dare suggest such a thing! Rebecca is going to be a ballet dancer, not a biker. The Sugar Plum Fairy does *not* have tattoos! And Cheese – I mean James – he's going to be a doctor. Why didn't you tell us you were taking them? We've been going mad!'

'Well, dear,' said Granny, 'we just happened

to be passing, and we'd bought these little helmets, and we were only going to be a jiffy, just once round the block . . .'

'. . . except we went round ten times because the babes liked it so much and your gran was in the driving seat and she went a bit mad,' grinned Lancelot. He whispered in my ear. 'She did a wheelie – with the sidecar and everything. What a woman!'

'I heard that!' snapped Mum. 'Doing wheelies with babies on board! How could you?'

'Oh it's quite easy, dear,' began Granny. 'You go into third gear and you have to twist the throttle really . . .'

'I'm not asking how to do a wheelie, you . . . oh!'

So we got the twins back. Sometimes I think it would be better if they disappeared for much longer. I mean, who looks after them most of the time? Me! I give them their food. I bath them and change their nappies. I do *everything*. I think I might go on strike.

4 A New Kind of Wellington Boot

I don't think our next-door neighbour is very happy about our mini farm. Mr Tugg is always complaining. Dad and Mr Tugg don't get on very well, especially since Granny ran off with Mr Tugg's dad. She did and, yes, Lancelot is Mr Tugg's dad. They eloped in a hot-air balloon and got married. I mean – she's sixty-five, and Lancelot is even older!

Mr Tugg is quite short and he's almost bald except for a little bristly moustache that wriggles like a caterpillar when he's cross. He has a kind of warning system for when he's angry (which is often). First he goes red, then deep red, then purple and finally he turns white-hot. It's very impressive, as long as you're not standing too close. That's dangerous, because sometimes he explodes.

Anyhow Mr Tugg came banging on our door today. He never rings the doorbell. He prefers banging.

'The Martians are coming!' yelled Dad. 'Quick, everyone take cover. Oh hello, Mr Tugg, fancy seeing you standing there. I thought that noise was a Martian invasion.'

'You think you're funny, don't you?' growled Mr Tugg, and his moustache went wriggle wriggle.

'Me? Funny? Oh no, not me,' said Dad, peering closely at Mr Tugg's face.

'What are you staring at?'

'Is it going to hatch, do you think, Nicholas?' asked Dad, and I couldn't help giggling.

'What? Is what going to hatch?' demanded Mr Tugg suspiciously.

Dad stepped back. 'Sorry, Mr Tugg, thought I saw a caterpillar but it was . . . it was something else.'

Mr Tugg was breathing heavily. 'My wife was giving one of her aromatherapy sessions this morning,' he began.

'Aromatherapy?' repeated Dad. 'That's where you sniff smelly things to make you feel better, isn't it? I sniffed my socks once but it didn't work. In fact I felt awful afterwards.'

Condition Red, and Mr Tugg breathed even more heavily. 'Mrs Tugg had an important customer and your goat wandered in and stood there smelling like a cowshed. The poor woman was so scared she ran from the house!'

'That's the trouble with goats,' said Dad.

'You never know what they're
going to do next.'

'She was only wearing a
towel!' roared Mr Tugg.

'Nothing but a towel? That's disgusting! I
have tried, Mr Tugg. I keep telling her to put
on a coat and shoes when she goes out, but will
she do it? No.'

'NOT THE GOAT, YOU STUPID
IMBECILE – THE WOMAN! THE
WOMAN WAS ONLY WEARING A
TOWEL!' Now he was definitely Deep Red.
'Can you imagine how embarrassing that was

for her? And then, and *then*, when I finally managed to calm her down and get her back indoors I discovered that your goat had been eating my wellington boots.'

'It was very kind of you to feed her,' said Dad. 'She gets so bored with grass.'

'My wellies were outside the back door. She's chewed the toes off them!'

'That's why we call her Rubbish. She'll eat anything,' Dad explained.

'Look!' cried Mr Tugg, holding up the chewed boots. He had reached Condition Purple now.

Dad examined the boots. 'Summer wellies! Look, Nicholas, they're a sort of mix of boot and sandal – just right for the summer, so your feet don't get too hot. You could call them *bootals*, Mr Tugg, or even better, you could be like the Duke of Wellington. He invented wellington boots, and now *you* have invented summer boots. They could be named after you – *Tuggals*.'

Mr Tugg went from purple to white-hot to explosion in about two seconds flat. It was pretty impressive. Mum had to calm him down, just like she always does. 'Come in and have a cup of tea, Mr Tugg, while Ron catches Rubbish. Sorry she escaped. I don't know how it happened.'

'I'll tell you how it happened,' began Dad. 'That goat was trained by the SAS, you know. She used to be their regimental mascot. They trained her to sneak behind enemy lines and –'

'Ron!' barked Mum. 'Go and get her back. Now.'

So Dad went and captured Rubbish, while Mum told Mr Tugg that we'd buy him some

new boots. Dad wasn't happy when he heard about that. 'We're supposed to be trying to *save* money, not spend it on new boots for that dinosaur next door,' he complained. He stood at the back window staring out at the animals. 'Don't know how we'll manage,' he muttered.

5 Nuisance Neighbours

We're going to be on telly! Mum got a phone call yesterday from the local TV station. They had heard all about the mini farm and they wanted to come and do a bit of filming.

Dad's gone even more stupid than ever. 'We're going to be big stars,' he said at breakfast this morning.

'It's only local TV,' Mum pointed out. 'Not Hollywood.'

'You have no ambition,' Dad answered.

'And you have no sense,' laughed Mum.

'I could be an all-out action hero in the next fantastic episode of *Star Wars, Part 3005: The Phantom Wellie-Eater from Planet Goat.*'

Mum almost choked on her muesli and sprayed bits across the table.

'That is so disgusting,' muttered Dad. 'Isn't that disgusting, Cheese? Do you see your mother? She's a worse eater than either of you two.'

'Sprrrurrrrrrgh!!' went Tomato, and her breakfast went twice as far.

'You've been practising, haven't you?' said Dad, dabbing the table with a cloth.

Mum had just about got her breath back. 'You? An action hero? You do know what an action hero does, don't you? They do *action* – lots of it. I bet you can't even do five press-ups.'

'Huh! No problem!' Dad threw himself on the floor. 'One, two, er three . . . gerroff, Cheese! Gerroff my back!'

'Horsey!' yelled Cheese, hitting Dad on the head with his cereal bowl.

'Now there's a real action hero!' laughed Mum.

'Thank you,' said Dad, getting back on his chair.

'I meant James,' Mum replied.

But Dad seemed to have drifted off into a dream. 'I wonder how that TV news team found out about us? And I'll tell you something, that Martian next door is going to be really fed up when he sees us on television!'

So this afternoon the telly people turned up on the doorstep. A cameraman, a soundman – and a reporter. 'Tamsin Plank,' she said, shaking Dad's hand. He was wearing dark shades and

he'd left his shirt half unbuttoned.

'Johnny Dipp,' said Dad.

'Depp,' I murmured. 'Johnny Depp.'

'Cool,' nodded Dad. 'I know.' He turned to the whirring camera and smiled. 'Call myself Dipp sometimes to confuse the fans,' he said.

'You certainly confused me,' said Tamsin. 'I was told there's a mini farm here.'

'There is,' sighed Mum. 'Would you like to come through? Please ignore my husband. He's an idiot.'

'I am not!'

Mum turned back to the reporter. 'How did you find out about our farm?'

'Your neighbour, Mr Tugg, he told us. We're doing a programme about nuisance neighbours – people who grow their hedges too tall, people with noisy dogs that are always barking, that sort of thing. Well, Mr Tugg rang us and reported you.'

Dad nearly had a blue fit! He certainly did an amazingly good impression of Mr Tugg exploding. 'He WHAT! That mealy-mouthed manky Martian? He's the one who should be reported!'

'We'd just like to film the farm,' explained Tamsin.

'Huh! I'll show Mr Caterpillar-Face. You can

certainly film out there. We have nothing to hide. Absolutely nothing. Could you just give me five minutes to get rid of the goat poo?'

'Poo!' yelled Cheese, crawling out from behind Mum's armchair with nothing on.

'He means "boo",' Mum explained. 'He likes playing Boo.'

'He's . . . goodness! There are two of them,' cried Tamsin.

'Two poo!' gurgled Tomato, appearing from behind Dad's armchair.

We saw the results on the evening news. It wasn't too bad, except that the cameras had filmed Dad calling Mr Tugg names, and Rubbish tried to eat Tamsin's microphone, and they showed Cheese crawling about and looking like one of the farm animals. There was also a rather odd notice written in big red letters on the side of the shed. It read:

As soon as the programme finished Dad looked at Mum and me. 'Stand by for Martian invasion,' he predicted. 'Five, four, three, two, one –'

BANG! BANG! BANG!

'I know you're in there!' yelled Mr Tugg from outside the front door. 'I am not a manky Martian. How dare you call me Mr Caterpillar-Face you . . . you big baboon!'

Dad rushed to the door, crouched down by the letterbox and shouted through it. 'I am not a baboon!'

Mr Tugg crouched down on the other side and soon they were at it hammer and tongs, yelling insults at each other. Then Mr Tugg tried to poke Dad

through the letterbox with a stick. Dad grabbed an umbrella and pushed that out.

'Ow!' yelled Mr Tugg. 'That's grievous bodily harm, that is.'

'You started it, you stick Martian.'

Suddenly Mr Tugg's hand and half his arm came through the letterbox and grabbed Dad's nose.

'Led go!' bellowed Dad. The twins started crying and that was too much for Mum. She pulled Dad away from the door and wrenched it open, which brought Mr Tugg flying into the room with his arm still stuck through the letterbox. He twisted his head to look up at her.

'Good evening,' he said.

'Good evening, Mr Tugg. I suggest you go back home.

When the pair of you are calm enough to speak politely to each other we might be able to sort this out.'

Mr Tugg growled and went back to his house, while Mum tore a strip or two off Dad. She told him he was childish and he was deliberately winding up Mr Tugg.

'It's his own fault,' complained Dad. 'He makes life difficult for everyone. All I'm trying to do is feed my family.'

'I know,' sighed Mum. 'You're the perfect father.'

Dad shot a look at her. Did Mum really mean that? Or was she being sarcastic? Could Dad tell the difference? No. But I could!

6 Disaster!

Big disaster today. It started with a telephone call from Granny to say that the yoghurt was ready for collection. I thought she was going to bring it round in the sidecar on the motorbike, but Granny said she didn't want to jiggle it about too much. She said I should wheel the twins' double buggy round and we could strap the tub into that.

'You've got time to nip round, haven't you, Nicholas?' said Mum.

'I was going to play on my computer,' I said.

'You can do that afterwards,' Mum told me. 'The yoghurt is more important.'

So I grabbed the double buggy and went round to Gran's. It's not far, but you have to go all the way down the High Street, which is a bit of a nuisance when you're pushing an extra-wide baby buggy. People get cross and scowl and shout at you.

When I got to Gran's she was waiting at the gate, peering down the road. 'I thought you'd never get here,' she said.

'Is something the matter?' I asked.

'No, no. No,' she protested. 'I was worried about you, that's all. Come on, let's get the tub into the pushchair.'

The plastic tub was pretty big. Lancelot said that he'd used it for making beer before, but it

was ideal for the yoghurt. He was sealing the lid
with some heavy-duty sticky tape. 'We don't
want it slopping over the top,' he said.

'It smells a lot, doesn't it?' I sniffed.

Lancelot and Granny glanced at each other. I
thought Lancelot looked a bit worried, but
Granny smiled and said goat's yoghurt always
smelled like that in the early stages. 'It'll wear
off,' she added. 'Is that lid on tightly, Lancelot?'

'It is.'

'Good. Let's get it into the buggy then. It's
heavy, isn't it?'

It was too. That tub seemed to weigh a ton,
even with three of us lifting it, but we managed
to get it into the buggy eventually. Lancelot got
the tape and strapped the tub to the sides.
'There. That should do the trick. OK, Nick,
you can take it away now.'

I set off back to my house. The buggy was
pretty heavy and even more difficult to steer, so

it was hard work returning along the High Street. Everyone seemed to get in the way, or I got in the way of them. Then I almost ran Mr Tugg over. He eyed me suspiciously. 'Do watch where you're going.'

'Sorry, Mr Tugg.'

He looked at the tub and asked what was in it. I told him.

'Now I've heard everything,' he said. 'Yoghurt. You be careful, sonny. You don't want to end up like your dad. He's a lunatic, you know.'

I gave him a weak smile. What else could I do? In any case, I was a bit worried about the tub because it seemed to me that it was beginning to bulge for some reason. Then the lid began to lift up and down and rather pongy gases escaped from beneath it. Mr Tugg pulled a face and backed away.

I thought it might be better if I got off the
pavement and pushed the buggy down the side
of the road. Hardly had I got the buggy off the
kerb when – **BADDOOOOM!!!**

The whole thing blew up!

The lid went spinning high into the air and a
great geyser of yoghurt went whooshing up into
the sky and then came splopping back down –
SHPPLAPP-A-LAPPA-SPLOSH!!!

Oh dear. Cars were covered. People were
covered. I was covered. Mr Tugg was covered.
There was only one thing for it . . . I grabbed

the handle of the buggy and raced for home
before anyone had time to recover from the
shock.

I hurled myself up the garden path and into
the house. 'How's the yoghurt?' shouted Mum
from the kitchen.

'I've just delivered it all,' I squeaked and headed for the bathroom to clean up.

Of course it wasn't long before there was a thunderous knock on the door. The whole house shook. I crept to the top of the stairs and peered down. Mr Tugg was on the doorstep. You should have seen him! He was plastered from head to foot with goat yoghurt. It was still dribbling from his nose.

'Hello, Mr Tugg,' said Mum evenly. 'Has Mrs Tugg been giving you an aromatherapy session?'

He was speechless.

Tomato crawled between Mum's

legs, took one look at Mr Tugg and burst into tears. 'Bad goo,' she sobbed.

Mum picked her up and comforted her. 'I think you'd better go home, Mr Tugg. You're frightening the children. Goodbye.' She shut the door, turned round and looked up at me. 'Mr Tugg appears to be covered in yoghurt,' she said. 'Any ideas on how that might have happened, Nicholas?'

I told her everything. 'What is it about this family?' sighed Mum. 'Everything we do goes wrong. Oh well, I don't suppose we've heard the last of this.'

7 Some Gorgeous Bottoms

Mum was absolutely right. We hadn't heard the last of it. She showed me the local paper this morning. This was the headline:

BOY TERRORIST (11) EXPLODES YOGHURT BOMB IN HIGH STREET

I'm famous! Well, not really of course; only down our road. The police came round and questioned me last night, but once they had worked out that it was a genuine accident there wasn't much more they could do about it. Apparently the yoghurt had exploded because Lancelot had recently used the tub for making beer. He'd left some yeast in the bottom and it had reacted with the warm goat's milk and that was it – BOOM!

I learned quite a lot about chemical reactions yesterday. I think that if science lessons at school were like that you'd be a lot more interested, wouldn't you? I mean, your science teacher might get covered in yoghurt! (So might you.)

The odd thing is that Rubbish seems to know. I mean, how could she? She wasn't there in the High Street when her yoghurt exploded, and she certainly can't read newspapers. It's almost as if she understood what we said to each other. She just looks at me now with an odd expression that seems to be saying, *How could you do that to my precious milk?!*

Anyhow, I might be famous in our street, but

I reckon Cheese is going to
be the really famous one.
We had yet another visitor
today, while Dad was home.
Cheese had
been
toddling
after Dad for
ages, saying,
'Wetbot,
wetbot.' Dad
kept trying to get

WETBOT
WETBOT

out of the nappy changing but eventually he
had to do it. He'd just finished cleaning Cheese
up when the doorbell went. Dad

flung Cheese on to his shoulder
and marched off to answer it.
Standing outside was a young
lady who squeaked with delight
when Dad opened the door.

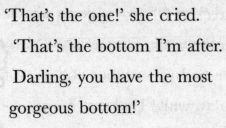

'That's the one!' she cried.
'That's the bottom I'm after.
Darling, you have the most
gorgeous bottom!'

You should have seen
Dad's face. He went red
right to the tips of his
hair and struggled for words.

'Th-th-thank you,' he said. 'Nobody's ever told
me that before. Erm, yours is nice too.'

The woman stared back at Dad. 'What?' she
said.

Dad stared at the young woman. 'What?' he
answered.

I hurried to the rescue and tugged at Dad's
arm. 'She doesn't mean you, Dad. I think she's
talking about Cheese's bottom.'

'Cheese?' repeated Dad. 'Really?' He stared
at her again. 'You want Cheese?'

The young woman hadn't got a clue what

either of us were talking about. 'Do I look like I want cheese?' she demanded. 'Why would I knock on your door and ask for cheese? I can get my own cheese if I want some, which I don't.'

'This is Cheese,' I offered, pointing at my little brother.

There was a long pause while the woman looked at Cheese, then me, then Dad. 'He's called Cheese?' asked the woman. Dad and I nodded. 'Why?'

'Because he smells,' Dad instantly replied.

'It isn't,' I said, and explained about Mum giving birth in the pizza delivery van.

The woman started to smile and soon she was laughing. 'What a very odd name and, oh my goodness, that conversation was so weird! I thought I'd come to some kind of madhouse.'

'You have,' agreed Mum, appearing at the door with toddler number two. 'This is Tomato,

Cheese's twin sister. Their proper names are
James and Rebecca.'

POO!

'Poo!' cried Tomato.

'No,' said Mum, shaking her
head. 'When you meet
someone new you say "hello".
You don't say "poo". Go on,
Rebecca, say "hello".'

'POO!' cried Tomato.

The young woman laughed. 'That's
all right,' she said. 'Babies are so cute, aren't
they?'

'Only when they belong to
someone else,' Dad muttered
darkly.

'Ignore him,' said Mum.

The young woman grinned rather stupidly.
'Well,' she went on quickly, 'I just happened to
watch a programme the other day about
nuisance neighbours, and I saw Chee . . . I

mean James, and I thought to myself, *That is the bottom I need.*'

'Oh no,' said Dad seriously. 'Cheese's bottom would be much too small for you. It wouldn't fit. I'd stick to the one you've already got.'

'Stop it!' hissed Mum.

'Oh, it's all right,' the woman giggled. 'He's quite a character, your husband, isn't he? I can tell.'

'Can you?' said Mum. 'Well, please don't encourage him.'

The woman giggled again. 'The thing is, I have a proposal that may interest you. I work for Dumpers, the disposable nappy people.'

I looked at Mum and Dad. 'We use them,' I said.

'We're looking for a toddler to head up our new TV advert. To put it simply, we need a beautiful bottom to show off our new range of throwaway nappies.' She leaned forward and peered at Cheese's backside. 'I've looked at hundreds of bottoms, but this child has the Mona Lisa of posteriors. We would like to use it in our advertising campaign.'

'Really?' said Dad, perking up considerably. 'Would he get paid?'

'Oh yes,' said the woman. 'Well paid.'

'Fine. Fine. What do you think, Brenda?'

'I suppose it might be a good idea. I'm sorry, but you never told us your name?'

'Jingle. Jingle Trinkett,' smiled the lady.

'Jingle Trinkett?' repeated Dad. 'And you thought Cheese was an odd name!'

'Cheese *is* an odd name,' chorused Mum and Jingle. For a second they looked at each other in surprise.

Dad put Cheese down as Miss Trinkett handed him a card. 'Here's the address for the studio. Perhaps you could come in tomorrow.' She bent down to Cheese. 'Bye bye, cutie-bottom.'

'And the same to you,' smiled Dad.

Honestly! I can't take

my dad anywhere. You should have seen the looks he got from Jingle and Mum. It was a powerful mix of flame-thrower (Jingle) with ice cubes (Mum).

I can't wait for tomorrow. We're going to be on TV! Well, Cheese is, at any rate. I might not be heading for film stardom but Cheese is, so I guess that I shall be the brother of a famous film star – which is almost as good as actually being one.

8 Lights, Camera, Action!

Brilliant day today! We went to the TV studio, in London. It was a huge building with an incredibly swish front. We had to give our names at the reception desk and wait for someone to collect us. There were loads of people coming and going. Dad reckoned he saw several TV stars. He even asked one for her autograph, and she was ever so pleased. She scribbled it down and then told him that actually she was only one of the cleaners! Mum couldn't stop laughing – not until she spotted Dan Crumble, the newscaster. That got her so excited.

'I can't believe it's him,' she whispered to Dad.

'That's because it probably isn't,' Dad

snapped back, scrumpling up his autograph and throwing it in a bin. 'I bet he's only the caretaker or something.'

But Mum went over and asked for an autograph and it really was Dan Crumble! Mum threw her arms round his neck and kissed him! Mwah!

'I spoke to Dan Crumble!' she said breathlessly. 'He kissed my cheek!'

'He's only a newscaster, Brenda,' muttered Dad.

'He's only a newscaster, Brenda,' copied Mum in a very mopey voice. She smiled. 'And you're only my husband, Ron.' She threw her arms round him and gave him such a noisy smackeroo of a kiss that everyone turned and looked.

'Gerroff!' shouted Dad, trying to look cross and waving his arms at her, but he got a fit of the giggles and they both fell about . . . My parents get more embarrassing the older I get. I can't take them anywhere.

'Kiss!' shouted Cheese.

'Kissy kiss!' echoed Tomato, puckering her lips.

'Go on then, Nick,' said Dad. 'Give the twins a kiss. There's a good big brother. Ah! Look, Brenda. Isn't that a charming sight? Big brother is kissing little brother.'

And you lot can stop sniggering too. Have you ever kissed a one-year-old? More to the point, have you ever kissed a one-year-old who recently ate a chocolate ice cream and still has slobby choccy mush all over his face? Yuk!

Luckily I was saved from further tortures by the arrival of an tall, thin young woman, who looked surprisingly similar to a telephone pole. Maybe it was her wiry hair. 'Hello,' she said. 'You must be here for the Dumpers trial.'

'Trial? I thought we were making an advert,' said Dad.

'Oh yes, but it's just the trial ad today, to see if your baby is good enough.'

'Good enough?' repeated Mum. 'Of course our babies are good enough.'

The young woman was flustered and she was turning red. 'I didn't mean your babies, I mean – oh! I'll start again. Today we are making a trial advert. We are trialling other babies too. Then we choose which baby we think will be best.'

Dad's head slumped forward. 'I thought this was going to be it,' he muttered into his beard. 'This was going to solve all our problems. But it's just a trial.'

'You will be paid for your time and travel costs,' said the young lady brightly.

'Oh woopy-doo!' muttered Dad. 'Rich beyond our wildest dreams, I don't think.'

Mum patted his knee. 'Don't get so down. It's not over yet. We still have a chance.'

I grabbed the pushchair and we all followed Miss Telephone Pole. We went through the security barriers and into an enormous lift and up several floors. Then we walked along miles and miles of corridors.

'We are now in the recording area,' whispered Miss T. P. 'The studios showing a red light above the door are recording programmes, so please don't make any loud noises. The big screen outside each studio shows what's going on inside. As you can see, Studio Six is where the news broadcasts come from. We shall be next door in Studio Seven.'

'Can I have a peep?' asked Mum. 'I got Dan Crumble's autograph earlier.'

'It is utterly forbidden to enter a studio when the red light is on,' warned Miss T. P., ushering us into Studio Seven.

Amazing. It was like another world. The lights were huge and brighter than the sun and so hot! There were three cameras on whopping great stands, and people everywhere – cameramen, lighting engineers, producers, directors, dozens of them! You'd never have thought it could take so many people to make one little advert for disposable nappies.

A big, cheerful man came rolling across the studio floor. 'David Dumper,' he announced. 'Head of Dumper Disposables. These your kids? Cute. Heard a lot about them.'

'Really?' queried Mum.

'Sure. Jingle was quite taken with them.'

Dad perked up a bit when he heard this.

'So, let's get down to work,' said Mr Dumper. 'We're doing a test shoot to see how it all looks on screen. We want a shot of your baby crawling across the floor, plus a second shot of the kid walking and wearing our latest product, the Bumper Dumper. Got a fantastic new jingle: *Oompah, oompah, stick it in a Dumper!* Isn't that great? OK everyone, let's get on with it!'

9 What Happened Next

Mr Dumper strode off, clapping his hands and shouting at everyone, while cameras wheeled into position. A make-up lady came over. 'I'll just get the little one ready,' she said.

'He needs make-up?' asked Dad. 'They're only going to film his backside.'

'That will certainly need make-up,' the lady pointed out. 'I'll powder his skin so it isn't too shiny . . .'

'Are you suggesting my son has a shiny bottom?' asked Dad, trying to look miffed, while Mum sniggered into her sleeve.

'No, but . . .'

'He's not Rudolf the Red-Bottomed Reindeer, you know.'

'Just ignore him,' Mum told the make-up lady.

I went with her to help keep an eye on Cheese – he is such an escape artist. Anyhow, we got him all powdered up, which he thought was great fun, and while that was going on Miss T. P. came back and said Mr Dumper  wanted Tomato to be trialled as well, so she came in for powdering too, and while *that* was going on Cheese was taken away to be filmed.

Things were happening so fast we didn't know where to look and it was all so fascinating, what with the cameras and the lighting and people shouting things like 'Take!' and 'Cut!' and yelling commands at each other.

They filmed Cheese over and over again,
doing exactly the same thing – well, it looked
like the same thing to me. Then Mr Dumper
asked for Tomato and they began filming her.
She was being a bit of a handful and kept
crawling off in the wrong direction. We were so
busy watching her that none of us realized that
Cheese had gone missing until Mum suddenly
cried out, 'Where's my baby? Where's James?'

Talk about a mad scramble! We searched everywhere, but couldn't find him.

Then Dad suddenly gave a shout. 'Some idiot left the studio door open. He could be anywhere!'

We stumbled out into the corridor but there was still no sign of Cheese. My heart was pounding – again. One day my baby brother would give me a real heart attack, and not just something that felt like one.

KEEP
SHUT

'There he is!' cried Mum. 'Look!' Mum was gawping at the big screen outside Studio Six.

Dan Crumble was sitting behind his desk giving out the news. What he couldn't see was that down in front of his desk a baby with a bare bottom was crawling past and gurgling, 'Wetbot! Wetbot!'

WET BOT
WETBOT

'Oh no,' groaned Dad. '*Here is the news: Cheese has got a wetbot.* This will ruin everything.' Before anyone could stop him Dad went crashing through the studio doors.

'But the red light's on!' wailed Miss T. P. 'You can't do that!' And she hurried after him.

Mum looked at me and sat down on a big, plush sofa. 'Come and sit here, Nicholas,' she suggested calmly. 'I think we'll just stay put and watch this little disaster of a soap opera unfolding in front of us. Oh look, there's a clown in the news studio . . . No, it's not a clown; it's your father. How could I be so mistaken?'

It was true too. There was Dad, striding across the studio floor, while Cheese went scampering beneath Dan Crumble's desk. Miss T. P. came racing after Dad. He dived under the desk to get Cheese, who somehow managed to scramble up Dan Crumble's legs and on to his lap. Cheese's cheerful face suddenly popped up above the desktop, while down below Miss T. P. had grabbed one of Dad's legs and was trying to pull him out from underneath.

'Hello,' said Dan, a bit surprised to find a baby on his lap.

'Wetbot!' cried Cheese.

'And that is today's news,' Dan went on evenly. 'We have a wetbot situation. This is Dan Crumble, Channel Half News. Good day.'

Miss T. P. finally let go of Dad, grabbed Cheese from Dan Crumble's lap and carted him off. Dad crawled out sheepishly from beneath the desk, pulled a pained face for the camera, stood up and followed her. A moment later Miss T. P. burst out of Studio Six and thrust Cheese back into Mum's arms. 'You'd better leave,' she said stiffly. 'You've caused quite enough trouble. Mr Dumper's had to go and lie down with an ice pack. Go on, go. Shooo!'

I grabbed Tomato and we headed for home. Nobody said a word all the way. (Apart from Cheese and Tomato who gurgled and laughed for the whole journey.)

10 Mrs Wobbly Green Jelly to the Rescue

Dad's down in the dumps again. He
says we can't ever get anything
right. 'The whole world is against
us,' he told us at breakfast.

'It's just a bit of bad luck,
that's all,' said Mum.

Dad raised a finger on his hand.
'One: we've been dumped by Mr Dumper.
Two: we owe the bank even more money than
before. Three: I've got a big pimple coming up
on my nose.'

'There's something else, Dad,' I began.
'Rubbish has stopped giving milk.'

This was true. I had tried to milk the goat
that morning but she kept putting both her
back feet in the milking bucket and looking at

me with an expression that
seemed to say, *No milk today.*
Milk's off.
She's
probably
stopped
because she
doesn't want any
more of her milk
blown up. She
was still eating

everything in sight. In fact she'd eaten one of
Tomato's nappies. (It was a clean one.) But she
wasn't producing any milk and, to tell you the
truth, I was worried. I'd grown very fond of
Rubbish.

Dad buried his head in his hands. 'Oh great,'
he muttered. 'Now we're all going to die from a
yoghurt famine.'

'Don't be so gloomy,' said Mum. 'Let's take a

look at her.' We went outside and stood in a little circle round Rubbish. 'See if you can spot what's wrong,' said Mum.

'Have you tried shaking her?' suggested Lancelot. 'Sometimes one of the bikes gets a blocked carburettor. If you blow down it and give it a shake it sometimes clears.'

'I don't think you can blow down goats,' I said.

'How about if I put her under one arm and give her a good squeeze?' he offered.

Granny punched him playfully. 'You daft clodpole. She's not a pair of bagpipes!'

A voice drifted across from next door. 'What's up with her, then?' It was Mrs Wobbly Green Jelly. (I gave her that name when I was about six. It's because she nearly always wears green and she's rather large – and wobbly, of course. I quite like her really. She's not at all like her husband.)

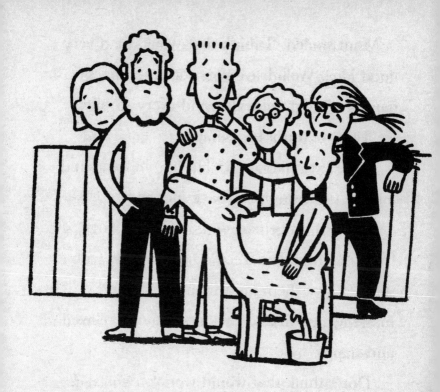

'She's stopped giving milk,' I told her.

Mrs Tugg leaned on the fence and studied Rubbish carefully. 'She doesn't look happy, does she? Maybe she's stressed.'

'Stressed?' repeated Dad. 'Are you crazy? All she has to do is eat all day and sleep all night. How stressful can that be? Huh! I'd love to have a goat's life.'

Mum smiled. 'I think that would be a very good idea. We'll leave you out in the back garden all night and day and every so often we'll throw you a few scraps.'

Dad's eyes narrowed. 'Ha ha,' he muttered and he went stamping back indoors.

'Animals do get stressed,' said Mrs Tugg, 'very much like us. People come to me with stress. I give them an aromatherapy and massage session and they go away all relaxed and happy.'

'Don't think that would work on goats,' I said, but what I really really wanted to say was, *Why don't you do it to Mr Tugg? He's the most stressed person in the universe!* But of course I didn't say it . . . Granny did.

'You should try it on your husband,' Granny declared.

Mrs Tugg burst out laughing. She did! She wobbled from top to bottom. 'Wouldn't touch him,' she chuckled. 'Aromatherapy doesn't work on volcanoes. It might work on a goat though. No harm in trying, is there? Shall I?'

I swallowed and nodded, wondering what I'd let myself in for – or rather what I'd let Rubbish in for. Ten minutes later I found out, because Mrs Tugg took us into her aromatherapy room. It smelled wonderful – a whole mix of different scents like pine forests and flowers and sea breezes. It was cosy and dark too, apart from all the candles. I counted at least thirty twinkling away.

Rubbish stood in the dark, looking rather lost and confused. No wonder – I don't suppose she'd ever had aromatherapy before. I stroked her flank and murmured into her ear. 'It's all right, Rubbish. You're going to have a massage.'

'Now then,' said Mrs Tugg softly. 'You come here, my beauty.'

Granny stepped forward. 'Not you,' laughed

Mrs Tugg. 'I'll do you later if you like. Let's start with the goat.'

I got Rubbish to lie on her side and Mrs Tugg began to massage her with lavender oil. After about ten minutes she rolled Rubbish on to her back and started to massage her stomach.

Mr Tugg appeared in the doorway. 'What's going on!'

'Ssssh!' we chorused.

'I don't believe it – you're massaging a goat! You're all bonkers!'

I suppose it did look odd. Rubbish was on her back with all four legs sticking up in the air and a blissful look in her sleepy eyes, while Mrs Tugg stroked her belly. She spent fifteen minutes working away. Then she said we should leave Rubbish to recover for an hour and after that we could try milking her. 'I've no idea if it will work, but at least we tried,' she said, fixing her gaze on Dad.

Dad looked straight back at her. 'Bonkers!' he mouthed silently.

But the thing was, an hour later I got Rubbish back on her feet, took her to our garden and put the milk bucket beneath her. I worked away with my fingers and soon her milk was flowing better than ever before.

'Hey! Come and look!'

Even Mrs Tugg was astonished. 'I never expected it to work,' she confided. 'I just thought it might help everyone feel a bit better.'

Dad went across to Mrs Tugg and gazed happily into her eyes. 'Mrs Tugg, you are a

magician. If only you could work your magic
on that old goat you live with . . .'

'Who's an old goat?' roared Mr Tugg, his
face appearing over the fence.

'You are!' Dad roared back.

'I'll get you,' yelled Mr
Tugg, trying to
clamber over the
fence.

Heaven knows
what would have
happened if Mum hadn't come rushing out
of the house shouting at the top of her voice.
'Come inside quickly! You've got to see this.
Hurry!'

11 Cheese Does the Business

You'll never guess in a hundred years – we've been on telly! Well, not exactly us. Just Cheese and Dad. There they were, on the news, watched by millions. They  were showing the bit where the news was interrupted by Cheese crawling across the floor. Apparently it wasn't the first time they had shown it that day either. There had been so many requests from viewers wanting to see it again they'd had to show it four more times. Cheese and Dad were stars!

Not only that, but Mr Dumper was on the phone almost immediately afterwards. 'That news item has been such a huge hit we're going to use the footage for the advert,' he told Dad. 'You and your baby are going to make a lot of money.'

The hallway was suddenly filled with song. 'Cheese has got a funny bum . . .' sang Dad. He came twirling into the room, pulled Mum from her chair and began dancing round. 'Cheese has got a funny bum, ho hum, a money bum!'

So things have turned out all right. I reckon we must be a pretty lucky family. We seem to have lots of problems and we try to solve them, or at least Dad usually tries to solve them but he just makes a big mess of everything and out of that mess comes something useful. Don't ask me how it happens, it just does.

Anyhow, Dad has stopped moping about the

house and he's even stopped complaining about all the nappies we get through because we now get free Dumpers, as many as we want. Dad was going to sell all the animals but I couldn't bear to part with Rubbish, so we're keeping her. Then Mum said she liked the hens and fresh eggs every day, so we're keeping them too. That only left Schumacher the tortoise, and Dad decided he was going to keep him.

'He's the best security officer we've ever had,' claimed Dad.

'Don't be ridiculous, Ron.'

'OK, Brenda, tell me this. How many break-ins have we had since Schumacher was put in charge of security?'

'None, but . . .'

'Exactly,' interrupted Dad. 'Like I said. He's the best security officer we've ever had. Anyhow,

85

now that I'm a TV star I shall need a
bodyguard and Schumacher is just right for the
job.'

Mum burst out laughing. 'You mad fool!'

'Foo!' cried Tomato.

'Foo to you too!' Dad shouted back.

'Wetbot!' yelled Cheese.

Dad stopped in his tracks and eyed Cheese. 'I
cannot believe that you have wet your nappy
again.'

Cheese studied Dad's stern face carefully.
Then he screwed his eyes up tight, clenched his
little fists, took a deep breath, turned bright red
and suddenly exploded with noise.

'POO!' roared Cheese.

Puffin by Post

My Brother's Famous Bottom - Jeremy Stro

If you have enjoyed this book and want to read more,
then check out these other great Puffin titles.
You can order any of the following books direct with Puffin by Post:

The Hundred-Mile-An Hour-Dog • Jeremy Strong • 0140380302 Winner of The Children's Book Award	£3.9
Return of the Hundred -Mile -An -Hour Dog • Jeremy Strong • 0141318430 'Breezy, daft exuberance' – *Sunday Times*	£3.9
Let's Do the Pharaoh • Jeremy Strong • 0141316820 'His books crackle with good humour and invention' – *TES*	£3.99
Krazy Kow Saves the World – Well, Almost • Jeremy Strong • 0141313749 'Superb . . . no udder book will do' – *Observer*	£3.9
Viking at School • Jeremy Strong • 0140387161 'A real talent for silliness and slapstick' – *Sunday Times*	£3.9

Just contact:

Puffin Books, C/o Bookpost, PO Box 29,
Douglas, Isle of Man, IM99 1BQ
Credit cards accepted. For further details:
Telephone: 01624 677237
Fax: 01624 670923

You can email your orders to: bookshop@enterprise.net
Or order online at: www.bookpost.co.uk

Free delivery in the UK.
Overseas customers must add £2 per book.

Prices and availability are subject to change.

Visit puffin.co.uk to find out about the latest titles, read extracts and
exclusive author interviews, and enter exciting competitions.
You can also browse thousands of Puffin books online.